Note to parents and carers

Read it yourself is a series of classic, traditional tales, written in a simple way to give children a confident and successful start to reading.

Each book is carefully structured to include many high-frequency words that are vital for first reading. The sentences on each page are supported closely by pictures to help with reading, and to offer lively details to talk about.

The books are graded into four levels that progressively introduce wider vocabulary and longer stories as a reader's ability grows.

Ideas for use

- Begin by looking through the book and talking about the pictures. Has your child heard this story before?

- Help your child with any words he does not know, either by helping him to sound them out or supplying them yourself.

- Developing readers can be concentrating so hard on the words that they sometimes don't fully grasp the meaning of what they're reading. Answering the puzzle questions on pages 30 and 31 will help with understanding.

For more information and advice, visit www.ladybird.com/readityourself

Level 1 is ideal for children who have received some initial reading instruction. Each story is told very simply, using a small number of frequently repeated words.

Special features:

woman

man

wife

Emperor

clothes

boy

Careful match between story and pictures

ening pages introduce key story words

Large, clear type

The next day the man came back.

"Do you like your beautiful new clothes?" he said. "Only clever people can see them."

Educational Consultant: Geraldine Taylor

A catalogue record for this book is available from the British Library

Published by Ladybird Books Ltd
80 Strand, London, WC2R 0RL
A Penguin Company

001 - 10 9 8 7 6 5 4 3 2 1
© LADYBIRD BOOKS LTD MMXI
Ladybird, Read It Yourself and the Ladybird Logo are registered or
unregistered trade marks of Ladybird Books Limited.

ISBN: 978-1-40930-710-5

Printed in China

The Emperor's New Clothes

Illustrated by Marina Le Ray

woman

man

boy

6

wife

Emperor

clothes

7

One day a man came to see the Emperor.

"I can make you some beautiful new clothes," said the man.

The next day the man
came back.

"Do you like your beautiful
new clothes?" he said.
"Only clever people can
see them."

"Yes," said the Emperor.
But he could not see any
new clothes.

The Emperor saw his wife.

"Do you like my beautiful new clothes?" said the Emperor. "Only clever people can see them."

"Yes," said his wife.

But she could not see the Emperor's new clothes.

The Emperor saw a man.

"Do you like my beautiful new clothes?" said the Emperor. "Only clever people can see them."

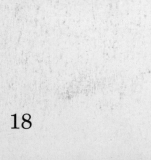

"Yes," said the man.

But he could not see the Emperor's new clothes.

The Emperor saw a woman.

"Do you like my beautiful new clothes?" said the Emperor. "Only clever people can see them."

"Yes," said the woman.

But she could not see the Emperor's new clothes.

25

The Emperor saw a little boy.

"Do you like my beautiful new clothes?" said the Emperor. "Only clever people can see them."

"No," said the little boy.
"You are not wearing
any clothes."

"Oh no!" said the Emperor,
and he ran all the way home.

How much do you remember about the story of The Emperor's New Clothes? Answer these questions and find out!

- Who came to see the Emperor?

- What was special about the beautiful new clothes?

- What did the little boy say to the Emperor?

Look at the pictures from the story and say the order they should go in.

A

B

C

D

Read it yourself
with Ladybird

 *Read it yourself with Ladybird — Level 1* — The Three Billy Goats Gruff

 *Read it yourself with Ladybird — Level 1* — Cinderella

 *Read it yourself with Ladybird — Level 1* — Little Red Hen

 *Read it yourself with Ladybird — Level 1* — Goldilocks and the Three Bears

 Read it yourself with Ladybird — Level 1 — The Enormous Turnip

 *Read it yourself with Ladybird — Level 1* — The Magic Porridge Pot

 *Read it yourself with Ladybird — Level 1* — The Ugly Duckling

 *Read it yourself with Ladybird — Level 1* — The Emperor's New Clothes

 *Read it yourself with Ladybird — Level 2* — The Gingerbread Man

 *Read it yourself with Ladybird — Level 2* — Sleeping Beauty

 *Read it yourself with Ladybird — Level 2* — Little Red Riding Hood

 *Read it yourself with Ladybird — Level 2* — Town Mouse and Country Mouse

 *Read it yourself with Ladybird — Level 2* — Sly Fox and Red Hen

 *Read it yourself with Ladybird — Level 2* — The Three Little Pigs

 *Read it yourself with Ladybird — Level 2* — Chicken Licken

 *Read it yourself with Ladybird — Level 2* — Rumpelstiltskin

 *Read it yourself with Ladybird — Level 3* — The Elves and the Shoemaker

 *Read it yourself with Ladybird — Level 3* — Jack and the Beanstalk

 *Read it yourself with Ladybird — Level 3* — Hansel and Gretel

 *Read it yourself with Ladybird — Level 3* — Rapunzel

 *Read it yourself with Ladybird — Level 4* — The Pied Piper of Hamelin

 *Read it yourself with Ladybird — Level 4* — The Wizard of Oz

 *Read it yourself with Ladybird — Level 4* — Heidi

 *Read it yourself with Ladybird — Level 4* — Snow White and the Seven Dwarfs

Collect all the titles in the series.